D0516304

Little Princesses

Princess Criseta's Hamster

Aleix Cabrera

Illustration: Rocio Bonilla

WINDMILL
BOOKS ™

There isn't **a windier** **place** than the Palace of Wind. Not even the hot air balloons can reach it, or birds to build their nests. The doors and shutters dance all day and squeak endlessly. When night falls, the noises grow louder, and Princess Criseta can't get to sleep until she is overcome by tiredness.

In the palace, everybody makes
fun of the princess for being so afraid.
"Criseta, the noise is our footsteps, the creaking
floorboards and the doors or... **maybe there are**
ghosts in the court! Ha, ha, ha!"

Only a little boy in the village

understands what her real fears are. Once a week, he goes to the palace with his parents to bring all types of supplies. Then, the two children walk through the mounds of rocks.

7

"None of the little animals you have brought me from the village keep me company at night," explains the princess to the little country boy. "Not the lizard, or the tortoise, or the parrot, or the goldfinch, **or any of the insects...**

They all sleep!"

"I bet you I've got it right this time!"** says the boy as he takes a ball of fur out of his pouch. "Here, do you want it?"

"A rat?" asks Criseta with a disgusted look on her face.

"It's a hamster," he tells her. "It sleeps during the day and plays at night."

Eek!

11

"I like it," says the princess. "But when I sleep, it will be alone and it will get bored. Bring me more."

"I don't suggest it, because they'll have a lot of babies."

"I'll look after them. Come on, bring me more."

"Take the pouch, there are three more inside."

Without saying anything

to anybody, Princess Criseta leaves the four hamsters in her bedroom. When it's bedtime, for once she goes without complaining.

"Daughter, are you feeling well?" the king and queen ask her, surprised.

Blurp!

Pffff...

15

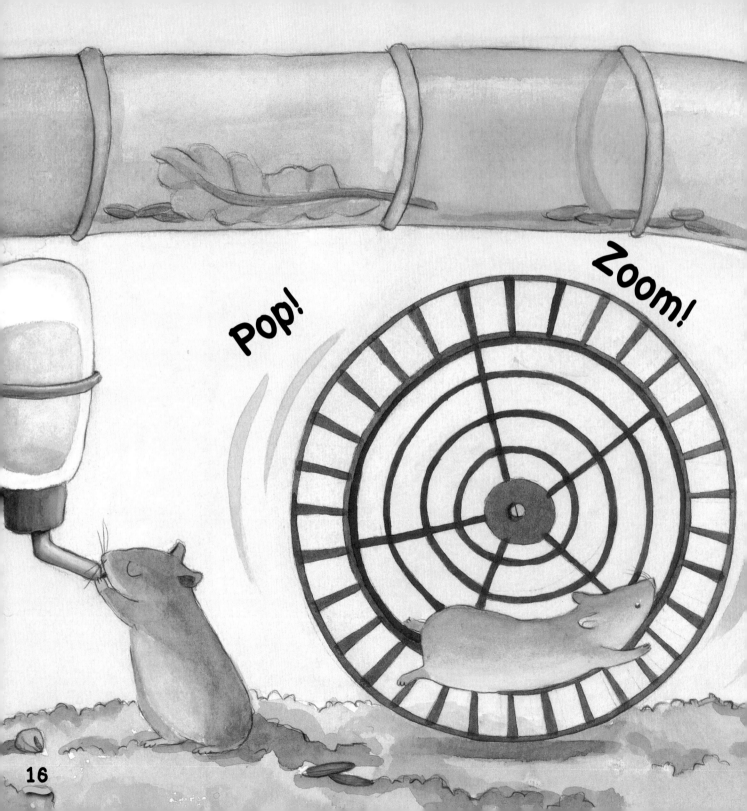

Every day, the princess waits eagerly for nightfall to return to the little circus of rodents. She likes watching them run around the colored wheel, balancing on balls, and **jumping from one side to the other until she falls asleep.**

But oh! Criseta

does not follow her friend's advice! After three weeks, thirty hamsters are running around her bedroom. "Oh no! You're going to drive me crazy!" she exclaims.

19

The princess decides to separate them and puts them where she can: **inside two jars, in the suits of armor, in drawers and wardrobes…**

But when night falls...
Scratch! Scratch!
"What's that?" shouts the butler.
"The wardrobes are speaking!"

"And the jugs are dancing on their own," says a cook.

"Did you see that basket running?" **exclaims**

the kitchen assistant.

Ooops!

Clack

Crack-crack! Crack!

"Suits of armor
that move on their own?"
asks the king.
"The palace is bewitched!"
says the queen, placing
her hands on her head.

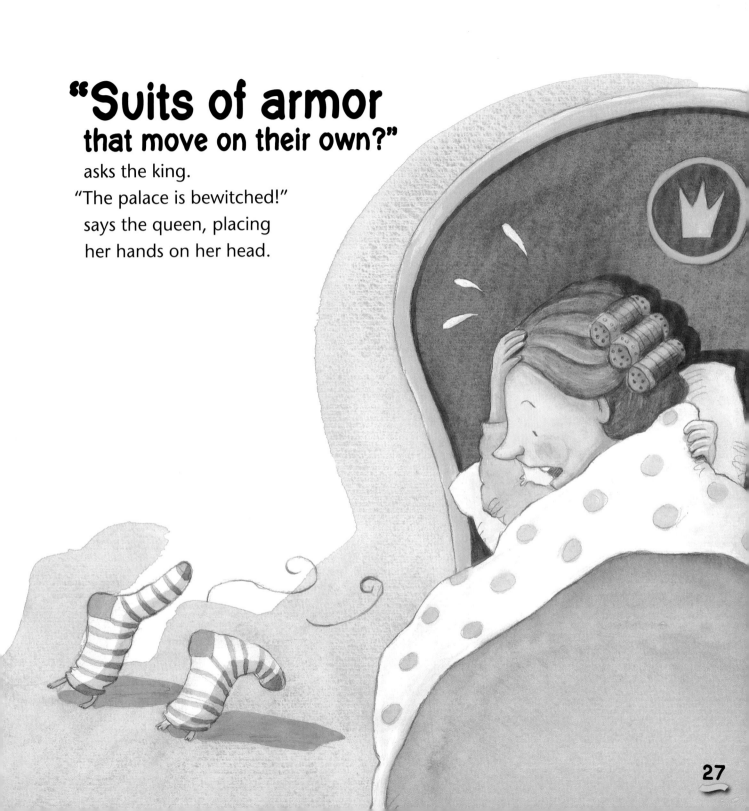

Princess Criseta hears the commotion and imagines the reason. So, she runs down the stairs to unveil the mystery and calm everybody down. "They're only hamsters, look," she says, smiling.

"Who's afraid of ghosts now?"

The little boy takes twenty-nine

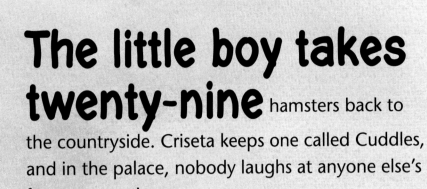

hamsters back to the countryside. Criseta keeps one called Cuddles, and in the palace, nobody laughs at anyone else's fears ever again.

Published in 2018 by **Windmill Books**, an Imprint of Rosen Publishing
29 East 21st Street, New York, NY 10010

Text: Aleix Cabrera | Illustration: Rocio Bonilla | Design and layout: Estudi Guasch, S.L.

CATALOGING-IN-PUBLICATION DATA
Names: Cabrera, Aleix.
Title: Princess Criseta's hamster / Aleix Cabrera.
Description: New York : Windmill Books, 2018. | Series: Little princesses.
Identifiers: LCCN ISBN 9781508194583 (pbk.) | ISBN 9781508193982 (library bound) |
ISBN 9781508194620 (6 pack)
Subjects: LCSH: Hamsters--Juvenile fiction. | Princesses--Juvenile fiction.
Classification: LCC PZ7.C334 Pri 2018 | DDC [E]--dc23

Manufactured in the United States of America
CPSIA Compliance Information: Batch BW18WM: For Further Information contact Rosen Publishing, New York, New York at 1-800-237-9932